Circle...
the Moon

by Barbara M. Lockhart
Illustrated by Kimberly Grunden

Peppertree Press

Sarasota, Florida

For information regarding permission,
call 941-922-2662 or contact us at our website:
www.peppertreepublishing.com or write to:
the Peppertree Press, LLC.
Attention: Publisher
1269 First Street, Suite 7
Sarasota, Florida 34236

ISBN: 978-1-934246-96-2

Library of Congress Number: 2008924693

Printed in the U.S.A.

Printed March 2008

So many shapes,
I just can't believe it!

Everywhere I look,
I see them, I see them!

Walking Path

Triangle, diamond, rectangle, square.

But my favorite is
the circle.
It is beyond compare!

My Halloween pumpkin is a circle, so is my dinner plate, the tires on Dad's truck, and the wheels on my skates.

But then there's the moon up there in the night sky.

I put on my P.J.s
and go straight outside.

Circle...the moon.
The biggest and
best of them all.

Maybe I can touch it when I grow very tall.

THE END

CPSIA information can be obtained
at www.ICGtesting.com
Printed in the USA
LVIC06n0837130518
577026LV00010B/90